A Junior Novel by Scott Sorrentino
Based on Characters Created by Andy Heyward,
Jean Chalopin and Bruno Bianchi
Story by Dana Olsen and Kerry Ehrin
Screenplay by Kerry Ehrin and Zak Penn and Audrey Wells
Produced by Jordan Kerner Roger Birnbaum Andy Heyward
Directed by David Kellogg

DISNEP
PRESS

New York

Printed in the United States of America.

First Edition
1 3 5 7 9 10 8 6 4 2

The text for this book is set in 12-point ITC Garamond.
ISBN 0-7868-4292-X
Library of Congress Catalog Card Number: 98-88404

For more Disney Press fun, visit www.DisneyBooks.com

Chapter  1

Brenda Bradford loved gadgets.

It was something she had inherited from her father, Artemus, who'd never met a remote control he didn't like. Like father, like daughter.

They were robotics engineers, and together they had started Bradford Industries, the largest manufacturer of robot circuitry in the world. But Brenda and her father were most interested in research and development, and for the last ten years their time had been spent on a single project: a part-human/part-robot crime-fighting man-droid. But this was no ordinary cyber-cop. They had gone out of their way to make sure that in addition to the obvious crime-fighting tools, their creation would be equipped with every gizmo, whizbang, and whosits imaginable. There were already over 30,000 individual parts, and they seemed to come up with new ones every day. The project had gone under many names over the years, but eventually Brenda and Artemus realized that there was only one thing it could possible be called: "Gadget."

The core of the Gadget program was a super-computer chip called the "Neuron Synapse Amplifier" (NSA, for short). It was designed to translate human thoughts into digital information that could be interpreted by a computer and used to control robotic parts. But it was much more complicated than it sounded. It was sure to be one of the great scientific achievements of the twentieth century—if only it would work.

It was getting late, and Brenda was tired. She and her father had been running tests all day long without success. But she was determined to keep going. Blowing a wisp of her auburn hair out of her eyes, she inserted the NSA chip into the special helmet her father was wearing.

Her nose crinkled slightly as she directed her attention to the foot that was positioned just a few paces away. Although it appeared to be an ordinary human foot, it was not attached to a leg—or to anything at all, for that matter. Instead, it just sat there all alone. Except that there was a soccer ball in front of it, waiting to be kicked—and waiting, and waiting.

"Come on, Dad, concentrate!" Brenda said, trying to sound inspirational.

Artemus Bradford twisted his weathered face as he

concentrated even harder. This was test number 752, and he had been concentrating for quite a while now.

Brenda looked at the foot again. Not a twitch. The most sophisticated piece of robotic engineering ever invented was motionless.

"I've got it!" Artemus suddenly cried out.

Brenda's heart sped up. She waited expectantly for his brilliant pronouncement.

"I think we should order takeout."

Brenda's face sunk with disappointment.

"I know I'm supposed to think 'kick,' but all I can think is 'quarter pounder with cheese.'"

Brenda knew better than to argue with her dad's hungry thoughts.

"All right," she said, grabbing her coat. "I'll get us some dinner. But then we keep going."

Artemus nodded and leaned back in his chair, satisfied with even a moment's relaxation after the long day. He switched on some music and turned up the volume. The silky tones of soul music filled the laboratory.

Brenda smiled. It was such a "Dad" thing to play that old music from AM radio, but if it made him happy, she was all for it. Now, where had she put her keys? Ah, there they were.

She gathered up the keys and her purse and was heading out the door when suddenly she saw an amazing thing. Her father was tapping his foot to the music. And the robotic foot was tapping. They were tapping together—perfectly in synch.

"Dad!" she whispered as loudly as she dared, not wanting to disturb whatever was making it work.

Artemus looked at her, then followed her gaze to the robo-foot. His jaw dropped in astonishment, but he managed to keep tapping his foot. And as he did, so did the robo-foot.

"The Neuron Synapse Amplifier! It's working!" he exclaimed.

Dr. Bradford was so excited that he began to dance. And the foot matched his dancing, move for move! Brenda watched for a moment, then joined in the celebration and the three of them danced together— father, daughter, and foot!

"I have to call Chief Quimby on Monday and tell him he can start screening recruits," Brenda said excitedly.

This really was cause for celebration. The Gadget program had now entered its final phase, and ten years of hard work was about to pay off! Go-Go-Gadget! she thought to herself, shimmying and shaking to the music.

"How about that dinner?" her father asked, not meaning to break up the party but anxious to feed his growling stomach.

Brenda smiled. "Okay, burger and fries, super-sized, right?"

Artemus nodded enthusiastically.

"Back in twenty," she said. "Don't wear out the foot, Dad."

As she turned to leave, her mind suddenly switched to a more practical mode. Recruits?

"Dad?" she asked, stopping at the door. "How am I going to find the right subject for our experiment?"

"Don't worry," her father answered confidently. "When you find the right man, you'll know."

Chapter 2

John Brown looked out from his security post at the perimeter of Bradford Industries. Fred, the delivery-van driver, was motioning for him to open the gate so he could leave.

John took out his pen and using the spring mechanism as a makeshift firing device, shot the ink cartridge across the booth, where it hit the green "open" button for the security gate. Perfect shot! But then the cartridge ricocheted, knocking over his partner Thelma's coffee before bouncing back and hitting the "close" button. John looked at Fred sheepishly as the gate closed on top of his van. Oops.

"Brown, go home before you hurt someone," Thelma suggested, glaring at him as she sopped up the spilled coffee with a napkin.

John wasn't sure how he had misfired so badly. Back home in Ogalaluga he could knock a can off a fence at forty feet with that maneuver. But maybe she was right. After all, his shift had ended five minutes ago.

Before he could entertain another thought, movement on one of the security monitors caught his attention. He zoomed the image closer and recognized Brenda Bradford leaving her laboratory. Her hair was mussed, held marginally in place with several pencils, and her glasses sat halfway down on her nose, but to John she was the most beautiful thing in the world.

"Wowser!" he whispered.

"What?" asked Thelma.

"Just talking to myself," he explained, checking his reflection in the window. He was what a lot of women would call "cute," which was fine when you were thirteen, but became annoying when you passed thirty. He turned to Thelma.

"How do I look?"

"Like a geek from Kansas who became a security guard," she replied bluntly.

"Is that bad?"

Thelma rolled her eyes. Sometimes he really wore on her patience.

John checked the monitor again. If he timed it just right. . . . He headed off into the complex. Thelma watched him go, shaking her head.

Someone else was also interested in Brenda Bradford's movements. She appeared on a twelve-inch monitor situated in the rear of a fashionably decorated limousine parked nearby. Its occupant, Sanford Scolex, fixed his gaze on the video image while his pure white cat, Sniffy, purred contentedly in his lap.

"She's left the lab," Scolex snapped at his chauffeur and number-one henchman, Sikes. "Now go get me that foot!"

In the driver's seat, Sikes, a larger-than-life man, sighed and got to work.

John had timed his walk perfectly, bumping into Brenda just as she rounded a corner on her way to the parking lot.

"Dr. Bradford!" he said enthusiastically. "Hi."

Brenda stared at him blankly for a moment, then looked down at the badge pinned to his breast pocket.

"Brown John," she said, reading. "That's an interesting name."

"Actually, it's John Brown. See," he explained, "there's a comma."

Brenda pushed her glasses up on her nose and took a second look.

"Oh, yes," she said.

They stood there silently for a moment, then John sprang into action. "I borrowed a book from your lab and I—I just wanted to return it."

"A book?" Her forehead wrinkled with curiosity.

"Power Learning through Speed Study," he said.

Brenda gave a slight nod of semirecognition, which was all the encouragement John needed to press on.

"Took me forever to get through it. I think it will really pay off, though. I just applied to the Riverton Police Force."

"Oh, congratulations," she said, only half-paying attention.

"Thanks," John said, continuing despite his nervousness. "It's what I've always wanted to do—help people, that is."

In fact, it was the whole reason he'd moved to Riverton from Kansas. And when he had first seen Brenda Bradford, he knew he had made the right choice.

"I guess it's sort of what you do, too," he added.

"Uh, sure," she agreed, though she had never thought of it that way. Help people? She considered this as they slowly walked across the parking lot toward her car.

She had always loved science and math—testing theories, solving equations. Not very practical, she thought. But maybe John Brown was right. Maybe the Gadget program *was* about helping people. As she finished that thought, they had reached her car.

"Well, here you go," John said, handing her the book.

"Thanks."

She tossed the book in the back of her car and

looked at John. He seemed like a decent guy, if a bit excitable.

There was an awkward silence as they took turns wondering who was going to speak next. Soon, John found himself looking at the sky, and without thinking he blurted, "Nice stars."

"Which ones?" she asked, happy to be talking about astronomy, one of her favorite subjects.

"I just meant . . . you know, the whole . . . "

"Oh. Sorry. I thought you meant a specific cluster." Brenda mentally kicked herself. "I always take everything so literally," she confessed.

"So do I!" exclaimed John, surprised to have found something in common. They looked at each other, sharing this new bond for a wonderful, albeit brief second or two. John didn't want to lose the moment. He swallowed hard, thinking how important it was right now to be sure and say just the right thing.

"Well . . . thanks for the book."

"Of course," Brenda replied graciously.

"And . . . maybe I'll use it again some time—" He paused. Did that make sense? "If it wears off or something." That definitely did *not* make sense. He had run out of things to say, but before it could become an issue, Brenda's attention was somewhere else.

"Okay, bye," she said abruptly, and before he could even offer his own parting words, she was in her car, driving away.

As he watched her go, he noticed something on

the ground at his feet. It was a pencil that must have fallen from her hair. He picked it up and was surprised to find it full of teeth marks.

She bites her pencils! he thought. With a contented sigh, John turned back toward the security booth. He was definitely in love.

Across the parking lot, Thelma looked up from cleaning the coffee stain out of her uniform to see a large black van pulling to a stop at the gate.

"If this is a delivery, you'll have to come back tomorrow."

The van responded by revving its engine.

Wise guy, Thelma thought. She shined her flashlight into the front of the van.

"What the—?" she exclaimed. There was no driver! Suddenly the van lurched forward, broke through the gate, and sped into the complex, heading for the laboratory. Thelma collected herself and quickly put out the call.

"All units! We have an intruder on the lot. A black van."

John heard the message crackle over his walkie-talkie.

"I'm on the case," he declared, just as the black van careened around the corner and raced across the parking lot, lurching wildly.

"Hey, that guy's speeding!" John shouted to no one in particular. "Ten miles an hour in the parking lot, buddy!" Then he realized—a black van! That was the intruder! He commenced his pursuit of the van, running as fast as he could.

Inside the laboratory, the back of the van opened and out sprang three ominous but cleverly designed robots. Tank, the largest of the three, was essentially a motorized battering ram. He was followed by Spider, a video probe, and Arms, a pair of metal claws. They immediately set to work breaking away the wall, and scurried into the lab where Dr. Bradford snapped out of his foot-tapping reverie.

As the robot trio entered, Dr. Bradford thought "kick," and the robo-foot sent the soccer ball flying into Spider, who toppled end-over-end into the corner of the lab.

Arms went straight for the foot. Anticipating the robot's move, Dr. Bradford lunged for the foot as well and soon robot and man were engaged in a serious game of tug-of-war.

But Dr. Bradford was no match for the robots. A laserlike weapon popped out of Tank and zapped the unsuspecting scientist. The high voltage caused the NSA chip to eject from the helmet at the same time it sent Dr. Bradford hurtling across the room. The impact knocked his helmet off, and it rolled conveniently to Arms, who grabbed it along with the foot and headed for the van.

Mission accomplished, the other two robots turned

and zoomed out of the room just as John Brown dashed in.

"Dr. Bradford!" he cried, rushing to his side.

Dr. Bradford tried to speak, but the electric shock and the trauma of his fall was more than the scientist could bear. Within a few seconds, his arms fell lifelessly to his sides. He was gone.

John bent over him in a state of shock. He suddenly felt a surge of anger inside. This was wrong! he thought. Whoever did this must pay!

"Rest in peace, Dr. Bradford," he swore solemnly. "You have my word that the perpetrators of this crime will be brought to justice."

The sound of the van doors slamming interrupted his heroic pronouncement and he ran out of the lab just in time to see the van skid around the corner. He watched Thelma try to block the exit, but the van swerved past her, out the main gate, and onto the road. John quickly ran to his car, a beat-up Chevette.

"Brown!" Thelma called to him. "Where are you going?"

"To catch the bad guys," he said, starting the car. He reached around to the backseat. There was his blue bowling ball, laundry, and papers—yes! The cherry light! No pursuit was complete without one. He slapped it on the roof and sped off.

Too many episodes of *Starsky and Hutch,* Thelma thought as she watched John race away in the wrong direction.

"Brown! They went that way!" She pointed frantically, hoping he could see her in his rearview mirror.

More determined than ever, John screeched to a halt, reversed direction, and raced down the road in pursuit of the van.

Chapter 3

Sanford Scolex examined the stolen goods from the comfort of his limo. He held up the foot, admiring the craftsmanship. It didn't matter to him that he had nothing to do with making it or that he had stolen it from someone else. All that mattered was that it was his now. His to admire and his to play with, and his with which to fulfill his lifelong ambition of global domination. The thought of it made him positively giddy. He played with the toes of the foot like a child.

"This little piggy stole a computer chip!" he chirped. "And this little piggy copied it! And this little piggy made a global robotic army and this little piggy got RICH! And the last little piggy made all the world leaders cry 'wee, wee, wee' and run all the way home!"

He stood up through the limo's sunroof and took a deep breath, happy to be alive and evil.

"Now that I have this," he proclaimed, reaching down and pulling up—Sniffy? Oops. Sniffy looked at him, nonplussed.

"Or, rather, now that I have *this*—" He tried again, reaching down with his other hand and this time pulling up the stolen foot.

"No one can stop me!" he finished triumphantly, the cat in one hand, the foot in the other. Sniffy looked around and saw something that might require his master's attention. He started meowing loudly.

"Hmmm?" Scolex inquired, then turned to see John Brown's little Chevette fast approaching.

"Oh, no," he said dryly. "We're being chased by the hatchback squad."

Scolex ducked back inside the limo and pushed one of the many buttons on his control console. Thick black oil instantly sprayed out of the back of the limo onto the street. John was too close to avoid it, and as his tires hit the oil the Chevette spun out of control and shot across an open parking lot to the right.

As Scolex watched the skidding car, he noticed that for some reason it was getting closer as opposed to farther away. It took a moment, but he figured it out. Since both the limo and the van had taken a right turn at the last corner, the out-of-control Chevette was inadvertently heading them off at the proverbial pass. This frustrated Scolex no end. If there was one thing he couldn't stand, it was clichés.

John Brown, on the other hand, had stopped worrying about catching the van. He had no control of his car and was headed at an alarming speed for a set of billboard posts. He assumed a crash position.

18

CRUNCH!! His poor little car smashed into one of the posts and flipped upside down.

Scolex watched with glee, which quickly turned to alarm as he noticed the billboard toppling over into the street ahead of them. It was going to be close, he thought, instinctively covering his head with his hands.

CRUNCH!! The limo had broken the billboard's fall.

"Splendid defensive-driving, Sikes," Scolex repri-manded. But before he could continue, a booming voice broke his train of thought.

"Attention, driver of the wrecked limo attached to the billboard," came the voice, amplified by an elec-tronic megaphone. "Come out with your hands up."

Scolex was becoming irritated. Who was this guy, anyway?

"This is Security Officer John Brown," the voice continued, as if in answer to the unspoken question. "I repeat, please exit the vehicle—" The voice droned on, but Scolex had already thought of a solution to this little problem. He popped his head out of the sunroof.

"Fine work, Mr. Security Officer," he called out, trying to sound sorry. "You've caught me!"

That was good news to John, because he still hadn't been able to extricate himself from the wrecked Chevette. He watched from his upside-down position as the man in the limo reached into his pock-et and pulled out a cigar, expertly snipping the end off with a silver cigar cutter.

"Here, have a victory cigar!" he heard the man

offer. Then he saw the man light the cigar and toss it toward him. That seemed rather odd.

"Just remember, smoking kills," the man added humorlessly.

That was true enough, thought John as he watched the cigar spinning toward him. It landed inside the hatchback and John got a close enough look at it to realize that the end of the cigar was actually a fuse!

This can't be good! was the last thing John thought before the Chevette exploded in a flurry of papers, laundry, and one blue bowling ball.

Scolex was finally satisfied.

"Well—that was a big bang!" he joked. "And I happen to have a 'big bang' theory: we won't be hearing from that idiot anymore!"

He smiled with amusement at his great wit. Just as he was reaching for the controls to close the sunroof, he noticed a strange shadow, which seemed to be looming larger upon him. Scolex glanced up just in time to see a blue bowling ball crash through the open sunroof, landing squarely on his well-manicured hand with a loud and painful *THWACK!!*

He let out a bloodcurdling scream, followed almost immediately by "MEDIC!"

He was still screaming when the emergency vehicles arrived.

Chapter 4

Nothing short of a miracle could save John Brown as he lay at the hospital in intensive care. He was covered from head to toe with casts and bandages, and there was nothing more the doctors could do for him.

Brenda watched as Penny, the security guard's niece, sat at his bedside. She was only eleven, but a very brave girl. Even so, tears welled up in her eyes as she spoke to her friend and guardian.

"Uncle John, I know you can hear me. Please wake up. Look who I brought to see you." She held up a beagle. "It's Brain."

Brenda watched closely for any response from the man who had tried to save her father's life and had almost lost his own to protect her work. There was nothing the doctors could do, true, but there was something Brenda could do, if they'd let her. She had already discussed it with the mayor and Chief

Quimby. Now she needed the patient's permission. Reluctantly, she opened the door to the hospital room and peered inside.

"May I come in?" she asked.

Penny, momentarily startled, shoved Brain under the bed and quickly wiped the tears from her eyes.

"Sure."

"I'm Dr. Brenda Bradford," she said gently.

"Yes, I know. Uncle John used to talk about you all the time."

"He did?" She couldn't remember ever meeting him before the day of the accident.

"Is he going to be okay? You can give it to me straight, Doc."

"Well, he'll never be the same," Brenda said. She watched Penny's face closely, trying to gauge just how straight she could be with the girl.

"Everybody changes," Penny said, holding back the tears.

Brain suddenly tried to crawl out from under the bed and Penny pushed him back with her foot.

"That's right." Brenda paused, then continued, cautiously. "In fact, there's a really, really big change your uncle could make—if he wanted to."

"What are you talking about?" Penny demanded.

"Well, it's new," Brenda said. "It's never been done before. But if it worked out, it'd be amazing. Its called biomechanical enhancement. We'd rebuild your uncle with cybernetic prosthetics."

"So my only living relative would be the Bionic Man?" Penny asked.

"Not exactly," Dr. Bradford explained. "He'd be a cop. The most advanced crime fighter the world has ever known."

Penny practically leaped into the air with excitement.

"My Uncle John? A cop?" she exclaimed. "Why didn't you say so? Uncle John would die to be a policeman. You gotta believe me."

"I do," Brenda said, trying to contain her own excitement. "But we need your uncle's consent."

Brenda leaned over close to John and spoke softly. "I hope you can hear me. You are facing a difficult choice. Please decide carefully. This will change your life forever. If you consent, I want you to give me a sign. A gesture, a noise, anything."

For a long moment there was nothing. No movement, no sound. Then, suddenly, a low guttural sound came from the bed, and Brenda's face relaxed into a slight smile.

"You're a brave man, John Brown," she said.

Penny winked at her uncle, hoping he could somehow see her through the cast. The sound Brenda had heard was Brain growling when Penny had deliberately pinched him. But what did it matter? The important thing was that Uncle John was going to be a cop, and Penny knew that she had done the right thing.

23

Chapter 5

Mayor Wilson and Police Chief Quimby watched the surgery from a theater above the operating room. They were amazed at how many doctors and nurses there were. And they marveled at the staggering array of surgical equipment: scalpels, sponges, hoses, tubes, a dipstick, a slinky, and several things the mayor couldn't quite identify.

"It's a thing of beauty, Quimby," the mayor remarked to her chief of police. "The future of law enforcement reborn before our very eyes."

"Yes, Mayor," Quimby agreed. "Columbo and Nintendo all rolled into one."

"He'll make you obsolete," she warned. "No over-time, no hazard pay, no blue flu, and he won't call me 'Evil Gidget' behind my back."

Quimby almost choked on his coffee. He didn't think she knew about that.

"What do I have on the Artemus Bradford murder?" she asked, turning to business.

"You've got a limo without a license plate," Quimby said. "A few scraps of metal from whatever it was that broke into the lab—" He squinted at the operating area. What was that they were putting into this Gadget fellow now? It looked like a sprinkler head.

"Do I at least know what was stolen?" the mayor asked, exasperated at their apparent lack of progress in the case.

"According to Dr. Bradford, a robotic foot."

Mayor Wilson shuddered. "What kind of cyber-freak are we dealing with?"

The answer was to be found across town in the underground lab at Scolex Industries. The person in question, Sanford Scolex, was presently trying on one of the new prosthetic hands his lab assistant, Kramer, had made for him.

There were several designs to suit Sanford's various needs: a white-gloved hand for the opera, a chopsticks hand, a club hand, and of course, his pride and joy, the all-purpose metal claw. Kramer had really outdone himself, and Scolex told him so, causing an outpouring of heartfelt gratitude.

"Oh, thank you, Mr. Claw, sir."

Scolex had decided he needed a devilish nickname, something that would strike fear in the hearts of his enemies. He finally settled on the simple, elegant "Claw," having decided against "Hook" (perfect, but already taken), "Captain Claw" (too Saturday-morning cartoonish), and "Mr. Evil Tongs of Metal That Will Spell Your Certain Death, Infidel!" (way too long, and not catchy enough).

"Sikes!" Claw ordered. "Bring me the foot!"

Sikes was sulking in the corner, jealous of all the praise Kramer was getting. But he did what he was told, and brought the foot and helmet over, setting them on the table. Kramer inspected them with admiration.

"It's amazing, sir!" he gushed. "And to have designed it all by yourself." He was truly impressed.

"I didn't design it myself," he admitted to Kramer. "I had one of your robots rip it out of Artemus Bradford's dying hands."

Kramer's face reversed into abject horror and shock.

"Hello? I'm kidding," he cajoled, flashing a phony smile. "Come on, Kramer, could you imagine me doing something like that? I'm a man of science, a helper of mankind."

Kramer was instantly relieved.

Chapter

John Brown awoke in his hospital bed in the recovery room, though he couldn't remember how he had gotten there. In fact, he couldn't remember much of anything at the moment. He sat up. So far, so good. Looking down at his body, he saw he was dressed in a hospital gown and black socks. He swung his legs off the bed and onto the floor. Well, the legs still seemed to work, but as he stood up, he found he had trouble keeping his balance.

He lurched awkwardly across the room and checked his reflection in the mirror. He looked normal. He felt his head with his hands. He felt normal. Maybe he was normal. Just then, one of his fingertips popped off and hit him in the forehead. That was definitely not normal.

He looked down at his hand and recoiled in surprise as various tiny devices popped out of his fingertips: an aerosol spray tip, a pair of scissors, a flashlight, a corkscrew, and a flame that emanated from his thumb. This was definitely weird.

"What kind of painkillers do they have me on?" he wondered out loud. Of course! That was it. This was a drug-induced hallucination, or a dream, maybe! Well, might as well make the most of it. Some of those devices did look kind of nifty. He examined them more closely and accidentally activated the aerosol spray, causing him to sneeze, which launched the tiny rocket that was built into his big toe. The small but powerful projectile tore through his sock and began ricocheting around the room.

John fell to the floor as the tiny rocket whizzed past his head, crashed through the little window in the door, and zoomed down the hospital corridor, finally smashing through the wall at the far end of the hall. Yikes! Maybe he couldn't wake up, but at least he ought to get the heck out of that room and maybe find some help! He stumbled out the door and ran down the hallway, fishing wire trailing from his left index finger. "What's happened to me?" he wondered as he turned a corner, running straight into Brenda Bradford.

"Oh, it's you!" he blurted out, relieved to see someone he knew.

"It's all right," she reassured him.

"I don't know what's wrong," he stammered, panic enveloping him. "I—I seem to be ill."

"There's nothing wrong," Brenda said firmly. "It's from the surgery."

"Surgery?" He had no idea what she was talking about.

"The experimental surgery for the Gadget program."

"Oh." Of course, the experimental surgery, he thought. That explained everything—NOT!

"You may not remember very much right now," she explained. "You suffered a major concussion in the explosion."

"What explosion?" he asked, though he vaguely remembered something about that. She explained what had happened: how his body had been reconstructed using the most advanced surgical techniques, how he had just come out of a long recovery period, and the fact that he was now a sophisticated network of tissue, hardware, and software. She saw the light beginning to dawn on him and summed it up as gently as she could:

"You're somewhere between a man and a machine."

The man who had been John Brown looked down at his hand with all the paraphernalia extending from it, and let out an anguished cry.

"Noooo!"

He was nothing but a hardware store! He had to get away! He turned and ran. But how could he get away from his own body? He turned again, stumbled, and fell right on top of Dr. Bradford. She smiled up at him, trying to earn his trust.

"Look, I know this is new to you, but your body is new and it will adjust," she assured him. "You represent a huge scientific breakthrough, and a huge opportunity to benefit mankind.

"You were designed as the first cyber-police officer for the Riverton Police," she continued earnestly. "You said you wanted to help people—this is your chance."

"I do want to help people," John answered.

"I know. You told me—in the parking lot." She gently prodded his memory. "Somewhere between speed-reading and the stars."

Nothing could ever erase that moment from his memory. He looked at her and nodded slowly. Gazing into her eyes, it was impossible for him *not* to think that everything would turn out all right.

"I promise, I will be with you every step of the way."

"Okay!" John said enthusiastically, and with that, his head shot up to the ceiling on a coil spring and hung there, displaying a huge grin.

Chapter 7

The first few weeks after the surgery were not easy for Inspector Gadget (the security guard formerly known as John Brown). In addition to undergoing rigorous physical training to master his new body, there was a huge amount of technical instruction from Dr. Bradford about how it all worked. And since he was a complex electronic machine, the manual was 5,000 pages long and completely incomprehensible.

Dr. Bradford had tried to explain how the Neural Synapse Amplifier worked, but Gadget found it all much too complicated. In fact, he didn't understand most of the technical things she said, but he nodded as though he did anyway. He found just being around her gave him a sense of confidence. He did understand that the NSA chip was the single most important component of his new body. Without it, Dr. Bradford told him, his robot body would not work at all.

Gadget decided this cyber-business wasn't so bad

after all, and he loved the thought of being a police officer. His favorite part so far was something he had dubbed "the Gadget Suit." It was a specially designed trenchcoat and hat, loaded with voice-activated gizmos. All he had to do to activate a function was say "Go-Go-Gadget" and the name of the device he wanted to use.

Today was suit practice.

"Okay," Brenda said, "let's give it a try. There are two guys robbing a jewelry store and you want to trip them up—"

"Oh, sure, lemme think . . . " Gadget said, trying to visualize the situation. "I guess I'd say, 'Go-Go-Gadget—Oil Slick'?"

Bluish ooze shot out of his left sleeve all over Brenda.

"Turn it off!" she shouted, moving out of the way. "The valve!"

Gadget located the valve and turned it off manually.

"Oh, gosh. I am so sorry." He made a mental note to be more careful with the suit.

"It's okay." Brenda said. "Now, if you wanted to clean me up, what would you do then?"

Gadget thought for a moment. "Club soda?"

Brenda smiled and nodded. Gadget looked at her blankly. Where was he going to get club soda? Obviously he needed a clue. She mimed using a hose.

"Oh, right," Gadget said, picking up on the clue. "Go-Go-Gadget—Hose."

32

This unexpectedly sent a heavy stream of water from his other coat sleeve. Now Brenda was soaked as well.

After several weeks of training, Gadget grew more and more adept at using his body and the Gadget Suit. He knew he was making progress when Brenda introduced him to the mayor and Police Chief Quimby. Everything seemed to be proceeding on schedule. But Gadget and Dr. Bradford weren't the only ones who had been busy. At Scolex's underground lab, evil was brewing.

Based on the information from the stolen foot, Kramer had made numerous improvements to Scolex's android prototype, Prometheus. His skin was more lifelike and the connective tissue stronger, although it was still light-years from the sophistication of Gadget. It would never pass as human, either, but it seemed to please Scolex.

"An android of this quality could have a myriad of uses," he mused, giving the machine a thorough examination. "Shock troops, kamikaze pilots, hit men—"

"International rescue workers, teachers," Kramer interjected hopefully.

"Yes, I was getting to them," Scolex lied. He grabbed the helmet they had taken from Dr. Bradford and placed it on his own head. "Let's see him in action."

Kramer shifted nervously—he wasn't sure if the helmet would work.

Scolex stared at his robot and concentrated, willing it to move. Kramer shifted nervously again. Scolex concentrated more. Nothing.

"Dance, you stupid robot, dance!" Scolex screamed at the android.

Sikes tried to hide his pleasure at Kramer's failure, but he couldn't resist making a comment.

"Thumbs down," he reviewed.

"Thank you, Roger Ebert," Scolex sneered.

"I was afraid this might happen," Kramer explained apologetically. "Your design is *flawless*, but it seems the control chip we're using isn't powerful enough to fully integrate his various parts."

Kramer looked at Scolex anxiously. He hated being the bearer of bad news, especially when Scolex was wearing his claw, as he was now.

"I see," said Claw calmly. Then he turned away. "Something got left behind," he hissed through clenched teach. It was getting hard to control his rising anger, which reached a fever pitch as he brought his claw crashing down onto the table— *THHHHWACK!!*

"Uh, sir," Kramer said, not wanting to seem to upset, "that was my snack."

Scolex raised his claw. Sure enough, there was a smashed peanut butter and jelly sandwich stuck to the end of it.

Chapter 9

One afternoon after suit practice, Brenda invited Gadget to a picnic in her father's exotic topiary garden. Gadget didn't know what a topiary garden was, but he knew he liked to be with Brenda, so he agreed immediately. Now that he was actually there, he assumed that topiary had something to do with bushes and plants that were clipped into specific shapes. But what did it matter? All he really wanted to do was tell Brenda how he felt about her. And that made him a little nervous.

Brenda was more uncertain than nervous. She liked Gadget a lot, but she didn't know *how* she liked him. She wasn't completely sure how he felt, either. She certainly didn't want anything to jeopardize their professional relationship. After all, she was responsible for him.

As they sat eating their sandwiches, smiling occasionally at each other, Gadget was suddenly aware of the awkward silence. He looked around at all the strange shapes. He had no idea what most of them were supposed to be, but he wanted to say something.

"They're really, uh, they're hard to describe," he said, struggling to overcome his nervousness. "But . . . they're beautiful."

"This is my favorite place on the compound. I like to come out here in the middle of the night in my pajamas just to think." She stopped herself. "Does that sound strange to you?" she asked.

"Strange?" he asked, not sure what she meant. It didn't sound strange to him at all.

"I hear that a lot, you know—that people think I'm strange." In fact, she'd heard that her whole life, but it had never really bothered her. She was always too busy working with her dad. But now, with him gone. . . .

"I hear that a lot, too," Gadget replied. "Wonder why," he said, smiling.

Brenda smiled back, and Gadget summoned some courage, sensing the time was right.

"Dr. Bradford, there's something I wanted to ask you," he began, but he was interrupted by his own hat, which made a low, rumbling sound.

"Excuse me," he explained. "Guess I'm a little nervous."

"Nervous? Around me? How could you be nervous around the one who made you? Especially when I think you turned out so well."

"Yes, but—" Gadget started again, then realized what she'd just said. "You do?"

"Oh, yes!" she exclaimed. "You're just—astonishing!"

That was it. John was so thrilled by this revelation that his hat not only rumbled, it practically boiled over! The LED readout blinked RESET.

"Oh, my gosh!" Brenda exclaimed. "Here, sit down. Wouldn't you know it, as soon as I say you turned out well, your circuits start overheating. That's strange. Your pulse seems abnormally fast."

"Sammy Sosa," he recited. "Batting .332 with a man in scoring position."

"This shouldn't be happening," she declared, slightly puzzled. "Your heart is a Narvik 7."

"My heart is a what?"

"A Narvick 7. It's the top of the line," she explained.

"You mean—I don't have a heart?" he asked.

"Well, just not a real one," she admitted. "But yours is much more efficient!"

John pondered this for a moment. "Can this heart be broken?"

"No," she answered immediately. "It's virtually indestructible."

"Oh," he said.

They sat for a moment in silence, then Brenda stood up abruptly.

"I've got something to show you." She took his

hand and led him to another room in the vast complex—a room that was completely dark.

"I was going to save this until your Induction, but—ta da!"

She flipped a switch and the room filled with light, revealing the most amazing car Gadget had ever seen: a vintage cream-colored convertible Lincoln with suicide doors—in perfect condition!

"It's for you," she announced. "It was my dad's, but I added a few little touches."

"You made me a car?" Gadget asked in quiet disbelief. "The only thing anyone ever made me before was a sweater."

She opened the door for him and he climbed in, awestruck. The only thing more beautiful than the car was Brenda as she leaned in and explained how the car worked. He was finding it hard to concentrate on what she was saying with her body so close to his.

"Its got voice activation . . . ejection seating, power-assisted metamorphic camouflage system . . . a tricked-out cardiohoming device . . . and a killer CD player."

Gadget could no longer contain himself.

"Dr. Bradford," he started again, "there's just one thing I have to ask you—"

"Just say 'Go-Go-Gadgetmobile,'" she said.

"Will you—" Gadget tried to continue. But he stopped, distracted by what she had just said. "Go-Go-Gadgetmobile?"

As soon as the words were out of his mouth, the engine revved, the lights blinked on, and the car flew forward, knocking Gadget into the backseat. The Gadgetmobile whizzed through the open door and onto the road leading into town, as Gadget struggled to get back into the driver's seat.

Weaving through traffic and dodging pedestrians, the car sailed along. Finally Gadget made it to the front seat and slammed on the brakes—which had no effect whatsoever! He stood up, putting all his weight on the brake, but the car continued on.

"Mommy!" Gadget whimpered in terror.

"I don't want no Momma's boy for a partner, Jack!" a strange voice piped up.

"I'm gonna die!" Gadget shouted.

"You ain't gonna die," the same voice said. "So sit back and chill, baby." The voice was deep, cool, and completely in control. "We're just taking a test drive on the freeway of love."

"Are you talking to me?" Gadget asked, tentatively.

"It's like that," Gadgetmobile said. "And baby, we need to talk."

The car continued on its wild ride, somehow avoiding potential collisions, while John pleaded for it to stop. He tried pulling levers, pushing buttons, but nothing seemed to have any effect. Meanwhile, the Gadgetmobile seemed obsessed with John's love life, making all kinds of suggestions as to how he could win Brenda's affection. Gadget felt odd enough talking to a car, but getting dating advice from one was where he drew the line. Finally, he noticed a lever marked AUTO/MANUAL. He pulled it to the manual position and hit the brakes, bringing the car to an immediate stop in front of a convenience store. Gadget checked to make sure all his body parts were intact.

"Mmm-hmm," said Gadgetmobile. "I think that cat is perpetrating some malfeasance."

John looked out the window and saw a man in a long duster coat playing with the lock on a car parked directly ahead.

"Time to do some good," Gadget declared, stepping out of the car. He approached the man innocently.

"Can't find your keys, partner? Allow me to help."

The man quickly put his hand behind his back, hiding the pair of broken handcuffs he was wearing.

"Yo, Gadget," the car called, trying to get his attention. Gadget waved him off and proceeded to unlock the car door with a picklock he produced from the end of his finger. The man was more than a little surprised.

"That should do it," Gadget proclaimed as the door opened.

"Uh, thanks," the man said, climbing into the car.

Just then, a second man came out of the convenience store carrying groceries.

Inside the Gadgetmobile, the radio news was describing the jailbreak of two convicts from Riverton Penitentiary earlier that day. Gadget, meanwhile, noticed that the man approaching was wearing an orange jumpsuit under his coat. And if that wasn't enough, the jumpsuit was stamped RIVERTON FEDERAL PENITENTIARY in large block letters. Gadget finally reached the obvious conclusion:

"I see you work at the prison," he observed. "I'm about to go into law enforcement myself."

Gadgetmobile rolled his headlights in disbelief, then clicked on his arrest lights and siren. The man froze, dropped the groceries, and suddenly took off running, while his buddy leaped out of the car and ran in the opposite direction.

"Hey, what's the idea?" Gadget demanded angrily of his car.

"We got us a couple of jailbreakers," Gadgetmobile explained.

Gadget pointed toward the running men. "We should inform these prison work—" he stopped in midsentence as it finally hit him.

"Wait a minute!"

He finally put all of the pieces together and nodded at Gadgetmobile. There was no time to lose!

"You take the driver," Gadgetmobile suggested. "I'll go after 'Stop-n-Shop.'"

Gadget peered down the street. The would-be car thief had a good lead on him. Time to put the Gadget suit to work.

"Go-Go-Gadget—Coils," he called out, and coils popped out of his shoes. "Stop, in the name of the law!" he yelled, bouncing down the street in heated pursuit. He had almost caught up with the convict when his coils slipped out from underneath him and he lost his balance, falling face-first into a patch of wet cement. He hoped Gadgetmobile was having better luck.

He was.

Stop-n-Shop thought he was home free. He looked over his shoulder as he ran. No sign of the car or the guy in the trenchcoat. He rounded a corner and ran smack into something extremely hard right in the middle of an empty sidewalk. Except it wasn't an empty sidewalk—it was the Gadgetmobile in full camouflage mode, *simulating* an empty sidewalk. The impact knocked the crook out, and he sank inside the car, upside down, legs sticking up.

Gadgetmobile chuckled contentedly and dropped out of camouflage mode. He wondered how Big G was faring.

There was no way Gadget was going to let this guy escape!

"Go-Go-Gadget—Grappling Hook!" he said, taking aim at the escaping convict. The grappling hook pitched out in a high arc and missed the guy by a mile, hooking around a potted plant on a nearby balcony. Gadget let out a groan. The bad guy was getting away! But then he watched in astonishment as the grappling hook automatically retracted, pulling the potted plant off the balcony. The plant sailed toward the street and conveniently landed on the fleeing crook's head, knocking him out cold.

"Wowser!" Gadget exclaimed to himself. "I'm on the case."

Picking himself up out of the wet cement he noticed that a small crowd had gathered. They cheered as he stood up, and a flashbulb popped from someone taking a picture. Gadget brushed off some of the cement and tried to look official for the citizens.

Then he repeated in a loud, confident voice: "I'm on the case!"

Chapter  11

Sanford Scolex sat in an overstuffed leather chair in his massive office at Scolex Industries, weary and frustrated. He looked down at the screwdriver he held in his claw and the computer chip he held in his hand. He was a billionaire, he was the owner of his own multinational corporation, he had acquired more symbols of success and material wealth than almost anyone at his high school reunion, and yet he couldn't figure out how to make this tiny little computer chip work!

He stared blankly at the news on the TV screen in front of him.

"In an incredible display of courage earlier this afternoon," the news anchor was saying, "Riverton's first cyber crime fighter heroically apprehended two escaped convicts."

Scolex stared at the image of Gadget on the television.

"Why, it's that annoying security guard from the

Institute!" he said, recognizing the face immediately. "So he's the lucky duck they plucked for the Gadget program. Irony abounds."

Sikes looked up from his dusting. "Think he remembers that night?" he asked.

"I haven't forgotten it," Scolex answered, looking at his claw.

The news report continued. "The soon-to-be-inspector will be inducted into the Riverton Police Department at a gala event tomorrow night at the Civic Center."

"Oh, now *that's* interesting," Scolex commented.

A picture of Brenda appeared on the screen as the commentator continued.

"The Gadget Program was created by the late Nobel Prize recipient Dr. Artemus Bradford and his daughter, Dr. Brenda Bradford."

"Hmm," he mused aloud, conjuring up a plan. "Woo the girl, destroy the creation, steal her technology."

He rolled the plan around in his brain for a moment and decided that it was good.

"Sikes, get my tuxedo ready," he commanded. "Tomorrow promises to be quite an evening."

Sikes laughed maniacally.

"And stop that at once!" Scolex snapped. "It's so clichéd."

Sikes stopped laughing and started sulking. Maybe it *was* clichéd, but it was fun, and he never got to have any fun.

"Ladies and gentlemen," the mayor began, "I want to thank you for coming on what will prove to be a momentous night. . . . "

It was Gadget's Gala Induction, and while the mayor was speaking, Gadget paced nervously back and forth behind a curtain, waiting to be introduced.

Where was Brenda? Gadget wondered. The show was starting and she still had not arrived. Tonight was absolutely going to be the night he would tell her how he felt. Especially since he had already tried once and failed.

"And now, I give you the crime fighter of the future—Inspector Gadget!"

The curtain opened, and Gadget was caught by surprise as a spotlight hit him and the band played dramatic music. An entire ballroom full of people stared at him expectantly as the stage began to rotate and Mayor Wilson waved at him frantically to do something.

Then he spotted Brenda. She was just walking in from the lobby. In Gadget's eyes she looked positively beautiful in her gorgeous satiny-red cocktail dress.

"Wowser!" he exclaimed, much to the confusion of the guests, who conferred with each other. "Wowser?" What was that supposed to mean?

But Gadget was totally oblivious to anything but Brenda. She spotted him and flashed him a smile that could have melted the polar ice caps. It definitely did something to Gadget. His head extended up and down quickly, then did a 360-degree turn, then another. A rocket came out of his hat and sparklers shot out of his fingertips. The crowd went wild. Mayor Wilson gave Gadget the "thumbs up" sign, thinking he had planned the impromptu fireworks display.

The only ones not enjoying the show were some of the police officers, notably Chief Quimby.

"Great for the Fourth of July picnic," one of them noted.

"Yeah," Quimby agreed. "Next thing you know, they'll promote the copy machine to desk sergeant."

But most people were enjoying the evening. Gadget had met several important guests, but none of them seemed genuinely interested in him beyond the novelty of meeting him. Then someone tapped him on the shoulder. Probably another politician.

"Excuse me, Inspector," he heard someone say. "May I have this dance?"

He turned and saw Brenda standing before him. She was a vision!

"Uh yeah," he said awkwardly. "Sure—you betcha!"

He followed her onto the dance floor and gingerly put his arm around her. "Let's see if I can still do this."

He began to dance with her, growing more confident with each step.

"You're pretty good!" she said, somewhat surprised.

"I was taking dance lessons before the accident," he explained shyly as they continued to dance, "in case I ever got the chance to impress this beautiful girl I know."

"How romantic! So, did you ever get to dance with her?"

"Yes," he answered softly, glancing at her.

"And was she impressed?"

"I'm still waiting to find out," he said, twirling her gracefully. She laughed.

"Not bad, John Brown." She was having a grand time.

"You still call me John," he said, touched.

"Well, there's still a big part of him inside of you, right?"

What a perfect thing to say, Gadget thought. He was in heaven. Extending his arm, he led Brenda into a wide twirl, then snapped her back against him in a single, elegant move. Several other women were starting to take notice, but Gadget had eyes only for Brenda. The song ended and Gadget finished the dance with a graceful, romantic flourish.

"May I cut in?" a voice said, interrupting the moment.

It was Scolex, handsome, suave and treacherous. He extended his hand to Brenda.

"Sanford Scolex. We were at Harvard together."

Brenda looked up at him, momentarily taken by his good looks. They shook hands.

"We were?" she asked, thinking she would remember someone so handsome.

"Well, I've changed. I was quite fat then. Perhaps you remember me like this," he added, blowing out his cheeks.

She did remember. "Oh—yes," she said politely. "How nice to see you again."

Gadget's mercury was beginning to rise. He had a sixth sense about this Scolex, and he didn't like what his sixth sense sensed.

Brenda turned to Gadget. "Inspector, I'd like you to meet Sanford Scolex."

Their hands met with an uneasy force.

"I'll go get us some champagne," Gadget said, excusing himself. But as he turned to leave he secretly detached his ear and left it on a nearby statue. The thin wire was long enough to reach the bar, and he didn't want to miss any of their conversation.

"I'm not surprised that you've become a famous scientist, Brenda," Scolex said when Gadget was far enough away. "You were always the most brilliant one in school."

"Oh," Brenda said, blushing, "I was just a hard worker—"

"I remember," Scolex continued. "I used to watch you wrinkle your little nose as you concentrated on your calculations."

Brenda was taken aback. "You did?"

"It used to take my breath away."

Brenda sighed, and from the look on her face, Scolex knew she was falling for the whole act—claw, line, and sinker.

Across the room, Sikes, dressed as a member of the press and carrying a large camera around his neck, was preparing to strike. The intended target: an unsuspecting Gadget, who was far too interested in the moves Scolex was putting on Brenda to notice anything unusual.

Sikes's camera was actually a portable rocket launcher, and he aimed it at Gadget, pretending to be taking a picture.

At the same time, a happy couple danced into Gadget's ear wire, sending it zinging back into Gadget's head with such force that he fell off his stool. The rocket, which almost certainly would have hit Gadget, instead ricocheted off a metal post and headed directly back to Sikes. Before he could react, the missile struck his camera in exactly the same spot it had left moments ago.

The force was enough to send Sikes flying toward a large tray of what was about to become (as soon as the waiter lowered his lit match) a flaming ice cream dessert. Sikes landed in the dessert about the same time it burst into flames—Baked Alas-Sikes!

As Brenda and Scolex continued their conversation, a group of pretty girls began to flirt with Gadget. He tried to move away, but they were bubbling over with curiosity and just wouldn't leave him alone. As Brenda watched them giggling and batting their eyes at him, she felt a twinge of jealousy, and quickly looked away.

"Now that the Gadget program is complete," Scolex continued, "it's time for you to go on and do what you were meant to do."

"What do you mean?" Brenda asked.

He took her hand gently, sensing that he would easily win her over.

"I was devastated to hear about your father," he began tragically. "He was my hero, and it would mean a great deal to me to continue his work."

Brenda was genuinely moved by the sentiment, and Scolex pressed her hand tighter, ruthlessly playing off her tender emotions.

"Join me at Scolex Industries," he said finally.

Brenda didn't answer right away. In fact, she excused herself politely. But later that night, when Scolex watched her say good-bye to Gadget with a harmless peck on the cheek, he knew what her answer would be.

Chapter 13

A month went by with Brenda and Gadget seeing very little of each other. Brenda had her new lab at Scolex Industries where she had unlimited funding and complete control over her research. Gadget, on the other hand, was the novelty of the Riverton Police Department. Before long, he had saved a drowning child with silly string, rescued dozens of pets with his telescopic limbs—everything but solve the mystery of Artemus Bradford's death. Gadget became so discouraged, he was ready to give up.

"I know I could help those guys with the Bradford investigation," he told Penny as he opened a can of tuna with his finger can opener. They were making sandwiches in his kitchen.

Penny placed four slices of bread on the counter in front of them as Gadget cut a piece of American cheese onto each with his finger saw.

"It's just that Chief Quimby—" Gadget stuck his

hand into the bowl of tuna salad Penny handed him and activated his power mixer. "He says the Bradford case is real police work," Gadget continued, raising his voice above the loud motor of the mixer, "and that I'm not a real policeman."

He scooped some tuna out of the bowl and dumped a large glob onto each of the sandwiches.

"Maybe he's right. Maybe I am just a publicity stunt."

This made Gadget suddenly sad, and he didn't feel like talking about it anymore. "Tuna melt?" he offered, changing the subject. Penny nodded.

He held the sandwich up and with the thumb torch from his other hand, heated it to a golden brown.

"I can totally relate," Penny said after a moment's thought. "Like yesterday, I wanted to try out for the intramural soccer team and my teacher said I wasn't good enough. So I'm not even gonna try."

"What!" Gadget said, his mouth full of tuna. "Don't take no for an answer! Go back and demand the chance to show what you can do!"

Penny smiled. "After you," she said wisely.

"Good one," Gadget said.

Gadget went to Chief Quimby the very next day and demanded that he be put on the Artemus Bradford case.

"What's your problem, Gadget?" the chief said.

"Every time you flick your Bic you make headlines. Be happy with that."

Gadget continued to protest, but the chief was adamant.

"Get out of my office," Quimby roared. "Can't you see I'm busy?"

Defeated, Gadget walked down the hall of the police station, his head low. He passed a poster with his picture and the heading I'M ON THE CASE! What case? he wondered.

Someone tapped him on the shoulder. "Hey, Gadget. I need some help!" It was one of the other officers.

"Really?" Gadget asked enthusiastically. "A new partner? Backup?"

"Actually," the cop said, "I was wondering if you could nuke my burrito? Microwave's on the fritz."

Gadget's hopes were dashed, but without complaint he activated the heating rod from his finger and stuck it into the burrito. Within seconds it was piping hot and ready to be eaten.

"This'll be perfect for the stakeout," the officer said. "Thanks, Gadget."

"Stakeout?" Gadget wondered aloud. "Sounds exciting."

"Trust me, it isn't," the officer said.

"Yeah, well, beats doing nothing at all."

The officer nodded, then turned to walk away. But after a few steps, he turned back again.

"Hey listen, can I give you a piece of advice?"

"Sure," Gadget replied.

"You wanna earn your stripes? Make your OWN case. Know what I mean?"

Gadget took the officer's advice. If the chief wouldn't assign him to the Bradford case, he would just assign himself. Risking everything, he snuck into the file room at the police station and pulled all of the evidence. There were crime scene photos, police reports, witness testimonies, but something else caught his attention: a tiny piece of scrap metal in a sealed evidence bag.

"Go-Go-Gadget—Magnifying Glass," he said quietly, and a magnifying glass slid down his hat in front of his eye. He could see something on the metal fragment, but it was still too small. "Increase magnification," he commanded, and a second glass slid down in front of the first.

Yes! There was something there. On the side of the small piece of metal were the letters *S* and *I*. What could SI stand for? Gadget wondered.

Chapter 14

Back at Scolex Industries, Kramer and Scolex stood on either side of a gurney containing the new, improved Prometheus robot.

"I must say, the likeness is really quite convincing," Kramer said proudly. "Still, without the chip . . ."

Scolex held up an exact duplicate of the NSA chip.

"I tapped into Dr. Bradford's private files and stole her research," Scolex admitted.

Kramer was shocked.

"Relax, Kramer," Scolex said reassuringly. "Now that Dr. Bradford's on the Scolex team, we share everything."

Kramer, perfectly convinced, took the chip from Scolex and opened the robot's chest panel to reveal a complex web of wires and weaponry. Right where his heart should be, however, there was a large glass bubble containing a live tarantula. Kramer snapped the NSA chip into place and closed the panel. Suddenly, the robot limbs began to move.

A low hum came from deep within its inner circuitry as the robot sat up on the gurney and faced his creators. Kramer was right. The likeness *was* convincing. Prometheus looked exactly like Gadget!

"Good morning RoboGadget," Scolex said to his new toy. "You've just been animated by the most complex computer technology in the world. What are you going to do now?"

"I'm going to kick some #?%!"

Before long, RoboGadget had wreaked havoc on the city. In a matter of hours, he had been seen pushing over phone booths, switching the traffic lights at busy intersections so the cars would crash into each other, and generally behaving badly. But everyone thought he was Inspector Gadget. The 911 calls were coming at a furious pace. Inspector Gadget had gone berserk, they said. He must be stopped!

Completely unaware of any of this, Gadget and Penny were driving in the Gadgetmobile, trying to put the pieces of Dr. Bradford's murder together. It still didn't make any sense. Why would anyone want to steal a foot?

"Maybe it's like *The Fugitive*," Penny suggested, "but we're looking for a one-*footed* man."

"Actually, I have a theory about the letters I found

on the piece of robot metal they found at the crime scene. I was thinking about SI, and then it hit me—*Sports Illustrated*! Isn't it obvious?"

Penny was having trouble following Gadget's logic.

"Take a look at this," he continued, holding up the most recent swimsuit issue.

"Whoa, baby!" Gadgetmobile blurted out, catching a quick glimpse of the cover in his rearview mirror.

"*Sports Illustrated*," Gadget repeated. "Street name: SI. And look at these models. Do these women look real to you?"

Penny looked at the thin models in their skimpy bathing suits.

"No," she confessed.

"That's because they aren't," Gadget declared triumphantly. "THEY'RE ROBOTS!"

"Uncle John," Penny sighed, "I love you, but I think you have some loose wiring."

"Word up, little sister," Gadgetmobile agreed.

"But don't you see?" Gadget continued. "They killed Artemus Bradford, stole his technology, and created a robotic swimsuit model. She can do anything, go anywhere."

Penny and Gadgetmobile could hardly believe Gadget's ridiculous theory.

"Well, what other possible explanation is there?" Gadget asked.

Just then they passed a billboard with a giant SI

logo and the words SCOLEX INDUSTRIES—WE TAKE ROBOTS SERIOUSLY.

"How 'bout that?" Penny said, pointing.

"Well, yeah," Gadget agreed. "That does make a lot more sense. But if Scolex stole the foot," Gadget reasoned, "then he must have killed Doctor—"

His face went suddenly pale. "Oh, no!" he cried. "Brenda!"

Gadgetmobile did a quick U-turn. There was no time to waste. They had to get back to Scolex.

Chapter  15

"All right," Gadget said, standing at the entrance of Scolex's impossibly tall building. "I'm going in."

"I'm going with you," Penny announced.

"I'm staying right here in the parking lot," Gadgetmobile added.

Against Penny's earnest protests, Gadget asked Gadgetmobile to take her to school. He had no intention of taking her with him into the evil empire. That seemed to contradict the notion of his being her guardian.

As Gadgetmobile drove off, Gadget set his sights on a window, high at the top of the building. He shot his grappling hook into the air, and it made a perfect arc, landing just over the roof of the building before catching the corner of an air vent. Gadget gave it a tug to make sure it was secure. Then, with one big yank, the cable retracted violently, sending Gadget whizzing up the side of the building.

In her office, Brenda was horrified as she watched the TV news of Gadget (RoboGadget, that is) and his continuing reign of terror. She couldn't believe it. He must have completely short-circuited!

Suddenly there was a banging at her window. She hurried over to take a look. It was Gadget!

"John, my God! What's happened?" she yelled, hoping he could hear her through the thick glass.

"Brenda, are you okay?" Gadget asked, his voice somewhat muffled. "Has he hurt you?"

"Turn yourself in, John," she yelled back. "It's not too late! We can fix this!"

Gadget was frustrated. He wasn't getting through to her. He decided to use his loudspeaker.

"Listen to me, Brenda!" his amplified voice boomed. "Sanford Scolex is a liar and a thief! You have to get out of there. Go home! Lock your doors! Whatever happens—I WILL FIND YOU!"

Brenda watched as Gadget gave his cable another tug, shooting him up out of view. She was upset. She was confused. After a moment's thought, she hurried out of her office and down the hall.

Gadget soared through the air, pulled by the retracting cable of his grappling hook until he executed a perfect landing in—an airshaft? He clattered down the airshaft, bumping and banging all the way, and landed at the bottom with a final, metallic *THUD*.

After a quick damage assessment, he crawled to an access vent and removed the covering. Cautiously poking his head down through the opening, he found himself peering upside down from the ceiling of some kind of laboratory. There were enough high-tech machines, worktables, and other assorted contraptions to confuse almost anyone. Then he saw it. There, in the middle of the room, sitting on an electromagnetic pedestal protected by an array of sensors, was the stolen foot!

"I knew it," he murmured to himself. He studied the intricate alarm system for a few moments. This shouldn't be any problem, as long as he was careful. He deployed the suction cups built into his shoes and executed a Spider-Man maneuver upside down across the ceiling until he was just over the foot. Then, carefully extending his legs, he lowered himself toward the pedestal, stopping just inches short of the foot.

In a room next to the laboratory, great pains had been taken to monitor the security status of the foot. There were temperature sensors, floor pressure sensors, motion sensors, odor sensors, audio sensors, as well as several video displays showing the foot from various angles. Sikes watched over all of this like a hawk. A tired hawk in this case, as he was fast asleep at his post.

Chapter 16

Brenda knocked on the door to Scolex's office for the third time. Still no answer. Well, she wasn't waiting. After her encounter with Gadget she had a lot of questions she wanted answered. She pushed the door open and went inside the office.

"Hello?" she called out. A familiar voice answered her.

"Sandy, is that you?" she heard her own voice ask. She whirled around and found herself looking at— herself.

"What the—" she stammered, surprised to be face-to-face with what looked like her exact duplicate. "You're me!"

Then she got a look at what the other "her" was wearing: a tight, revealing outfit, and more makeup than she would wear in a year. "Sanford, you sick puppy!" she muttered.

"We're, like, totally twins!" her duplicate noted perkily. "We probably share brain waves!"

Brenda doubted that very much.

"You—you're an android," Brenda blurted, stating the only possible explanation.

"Sandy calls me his basic pleasure unit," the RoboBrenda confirmed.

"Pleasure unit? Eeeew!"

"I don't know, I kind of like him," RoboBrenda admitted. "Sure, he's not always really nice and stuff," she explained, using her natural gift for language, "but he's really rich and I like the way he dresses."

Brenda turned and ran. This was all just a little too weird for her and she had to find Gadget. The last time she had seen him he was hanging from the roof. She headed in that direction, with RoboBrenda running along behind.

With his Wire Clipper Finger, Gadget had successfully disconnected all but one of the sensor wires protecting the foot. As he concentrated on the last wire, he felt a bead of sweat forming on his brow. Even that could be enough to set off the alarm, he thought, but he didn't have a free hand at the moment. As the droplet made its way across his face, a hand extended conveniently from his hat and neatly wiped his face with a handkerchief before it could drip.

John breathed a sigh of relief, and with a quick

SNIP, the last wire was disconnected. He reached down and carefully lifted the foot from the pedestal, holding it in his arms.

"Gotcha!" he said with a satisfied smile. Only this was one of those times where it would have been better for him to keep his mouth shut. Voice sensor!

WHOOP! WHOOP! WHOOP! The sudden alarm caught him by surprise, breaking his concentration. His legs quickly retracted, knocking him into the ceiling, *WHAM*, and knocking the suction cups loose. He hit the floor with a *THUD*.

In the security room, Sikes awoke with a start.

"I didn't do it!" he yelled automatically, before he even knew what was happening. He looked at the monitors and saw Gadget running around the lab, frantically searching for the exit. He pushed one of the control buttons.

"Computer, seal the lab," he instructed.

Gadget spotted the exit just in time to see the large glass doors start to close.

"Go-Go-Gadget—Blades!" he commanded, and his shoes sprouted sleek Rollerblades powered by tiny rocket engines.

"We've got a blader!" Sikes's voice boomed over the PA system as Gadget streaked toward the rapidly closing door. "Repeat: We have a blader!"

Gadget zipped toward the exit, but the doors were closing too fast and he knew he was in big trouble!

"Go-Go-Gadget—Brakes!" he commanded.

Well, it was worth a shot, he thought as he crashed through the glass directly into the warpath of Tank and Spider, those lovable robots that killed Dr. Bradford. "Uh-oh," was all he had time to think before Tank zapped him with a ten-thousand-volt handshake, knocking him unconscious against the wall.

Brenda made it to the roof just as the alarms started blaring. She took a brave glance over the edge. It was a *very* long way down.

"John!" she called.

RoboBrenda was late arriving, but not even high heels could prevent her from pursuing her new best friend.

"This is so much more cool than that lab," RoboBrenda babbled. "All Sandy ever wants to do is talk about that gross foot—"

"Foot?" Brenda repeated, suddenly taking an interest in what RoboBrenda was saying.

"The one he stole," she explained simply. "The one he copied to make me."

Suddenly everything clicked into place. Gadget wasn't malfunctioning, he was right. Scolex had killed her father!

"Look at me, Brenda!"

Brenda looked up just in time to see her brainless alter ego cartwheeling toward the edge of the roof, singing and laughing giddily.

"I'm programmed to be a cheerleader!" she said, continuing to cartwheel. "I hope my underwear isn't showing."

"Watch out!" Brenda shouted, but it was too late. RoboBrenda ran out of roof, cartwheeling right over the edge.

Chapter 17

Gadget awoke to find himself strapped to a table. His hat and coat had been removed and Kramer, under orders from Scolex, had reluctantly opened his chest cavity, exposing his complex insides. Scolex was leaning over him as Gadget brought his eyes into focus.

"Hello, Inspector," said Scolex. "Nice of you to drop in."

"I owe you one, Scolex," Gadget said through gritted teeth. "You blew me up and my Chevette, too. And I liked that car."

"And you're the one who crushed my hand," Scolex snapped back, "and I liked that hand."

"Whatever you're up to, Scolex, you'll never get away with it." Gadget declared with more confidence than was warranted given his current situation.

"How cliché, Inspector!" Scolex scolded him. "You've been watching too many Saturday morning cartoons. Unfortunately, Gadget, in real life, evil quite often prevails." And to prove it, Scolex rotated Gadget's table to provide him with a view of the TV, where RoboGadget was running amok on a live news broadcast. Gadget stared at the screen, aghast.

"Hey, he—he looks like me!"

"Of course he does," Scolex agreed. "That's the beauty of robots: once you make one," he explained, "you can make a million just like it!"

"I'm not a robot!" Gadget protested.

"Ooh, somebody has a sore spot!" Scolex gloated.

"I don't get it," Gadget said. "Why would you do this?"

"To make teachers!" Kramer burst in defensively.

"Oh, shut up!" Scolex reprimanded him. Kramer was starting to get on his nerves. He turned to Gadget, savoring the moment that all evil geniuses savor: the moment they reveal their brilliant master plan to their helpless enemy.

"Why?" Scolex began, rubbing his chin. "To make techno-warriors that never get tired, never get hungry, and never say no," he explained with relish. "Every army in the world will be made up of my creations. Imagine the perks," he mused, "fame, fortune, floor seats at Bulls games—*comprende?*"

"I *comprende*, all right," Gadget snorted. He *comprende*'d all too well.

"Comprend-O," Scolex corrected. "Conjugate the verb, for pity's sake!" Then he turned to Kramer. "Pull the NSA chip," he ordered, "before he butchers another language."

Kramer laughed weakly, hoping it was a joke. "You're kidding, right?" he asked nervously.

"This time, no," Scolex said icily, confirming Gadget's worst fears. "I want to make sure no one else can develop their own android."

"This really wasn't in my job description," Kramer quietly protested.

"Do it!" Scolex barked, holding up a menacing claw. "Or you'll be building yourself a new head!"

Kramer reached into Gadget's chest and fumbled around, trying not to look at what he was doing and humming nervously. Then he fainted.

"Oh, good God!" Scolex said, rolling his eyes. He stepped over his fallen assistant, reached in and removed the chip himself.

Gadget felt the life draining out of his body as his vision faded to black. The last thing he saw was Scolex's claw smashing the NSA chip into a million pieces.

Chapter

Brenda arrived at Gadget's house just in time to catch a ride with Penny and Brain in Gadgetmobile. They hadn't seen Gadget either, so they decided to activate Gadgetmobile's homing device. It was a very weak signal, but it eventually led them to a junkyard filled with mountains of industrial scrap metal. It wasn't long before Penny spotted her uncle John lying in a pile of auto parts.

Brenda performed a quick examination, opening up Gadget's chest panel and checking inside.

Her face turned suddenly pale. "The NSA chip," she said sadly. "It's gone."

Penny didn't understand. "Aren't you going to do something?" she asked.

"The chip's gone," Brenda explained. "There's nothing I can do."

"What do you mean?" Penny cried, tears welling up in her eyes. "You *made* him, you *fix* him!"

"I'm sorry, Penny," Brenda said, placing a gentle hand on the little girl's shoulder. "Science can only take him so far."

As they both sat crying, Brenda's thoughts turned to the night of Gadget's Gala Induction. She began to sing the song they had danced to. Then she placed a farewell kiss on Gadget's lifeless cheek and motioned to Penny that it was time to go.

As they started to leave they heard a faint melody coming from Gadget. Something inside him had picked up Brenda's tune.

Brenda rushed back to his side. "John?! Can you hear us?" she asked, leaning close to his face.

Amazingly, his eyes fluttered open!

"Brenda?" he whispered hoarsely.

He was alive!

Brenda yelled to Gadgetmobile, who was so happy he had to activate his headlight wipers to brush away the tears of joy.

Penny threw her arms around her uncle, hugging and squeezing him. Not to be left out, Brain licked his face thoroughly, trying not to miss a single spot.

Brenda couldn't understand how Gadget could function without the NSA chip. "It looks like—your own body is making the connection that was broken when they took the chip. It's organic regeneration!" Brenda stood up and started coaching. "Come on, John Brown!" she yelled encouragingly. "Try to move your arm."

"I can't—I can't."

"Try," she insisted.

"You're standing on my sleeve."

"Oops!" She moved. "Now can you move it?" He was just barely able to do so. "Good!" she said. "Can you work one of your gadgets?"

Slowly, the top of his head started to creak open.

"That's it," she coaxed. "Come on."

The rocket launcher creaked into position.

"Good. Now fire it, John. You can do it yourself!"

"C'mon, baby" added Gadgetmobile.

"C'mon, Uncle John!" Penny joined in. Gadget gritted his teeth. A tiny flare frizzled out, emitting a high-pitched whistle, smoke trailing from its tail. It whizzed by erratically, then exploded in a miniature fireworks display.

Chapter 19

At the other end of the city, Chief Quimby was on the phone with the mayor when RoboGadget exploded through his door and sprayed his desk with a blast of fire from his sleeve.

"If this is about the other day," Quimby said, trying to be casual, "that was just the job talking. Truth is, I would love to have you on the Bradford case."

A whirling corkscrew rotated out of RoboGadget's finger as he grabbed the chief by the collar.

"Do you have any idea how painful it is to have a corkscrew drilled into your brain?" RoboGadget inquired.

Just then, a group of cops rushed into the office, weapons at the ready. RoboGadget dropped the chief and started spraying them with fire. But the odds were against him, so he jumped out the window in a spray of broken glass and ran off down the street.

"Mayor," Quimby spoke calmly into the phone, "just one question—WHERE'S THE OFF SWITCH?!"

Brenda was using electricity from Gadgetmobile to recharge Gadget, but it wasn't entirely working. After pondering the problem for a moment, Gadgetmobile came up with a suggestion: "You've got to jump-start your soul." Penny agreed and encouraged her uncle John to sing. Gadgetmobile tried to get him started with a soul tune, but Gadget couldn't feel the groove.

"Come on, Uncle John," Penny instructed, "pretend you're in the shower. Sing *your* song."

He started to protest, but Brenda cut him off.

"It worked for my father," she stated firmly.

So Gadget began to sing—hesitantly at first, but growing stronger with each note. Not to be left out, Brain began to howl along. Soon the whole junkyard was filled with the sound of music, inspiring Gadget to leap to his feet. He finished his song with a sustained high note, a twirl, and a knee slide.

"You're right," he said, joyfully filling his lungs with polluted gray junkyard air. "I feel much better!" Then every gadget in him extended, twirled, and settled back in place triumphantly.

Meanwhile, RoboGadget was amusing himself by terrorizing the citizens of Riverton with his Godzilla shadow puppet—until Scolex found him and busted him.

"Get in the car!" Scolex ordered his evil creation.

"Just five more minutes," RoboGadget whined.

"NOW!" roared Scolex. RoboGadget did as he was told, and they sped off.

Having fully checked his systems, Gadget was ready to go. He and the others piled into Gadgetmobile.

"Y'all better buckle up now, ya hear," warned Gadgetmobile as a rocket booster popped out of his trunk. The rocket fired and the car streaked away as fast as lightning.

First, Penny and Brain were dropped off at their doorstep.

"If I'm home late," Gadget called to them from the car, "it just means it took a little extra time to over-throw Scolex's evil empire, okay?"

Penny smiled for her uncle and waved good-bye as Gadget and Brenda sped off in the Gadgetmobile to stop Scolex once and for all!

Chapter  20

They spotted Scolex's limo on the way to the bridge leading from the city to Scolex Industries. Gadgetmobile pulled up behind as Gadget launched himself through the window into the limo's backseat.

"You're under arrest for the murder of Dr. Artemus Bradford," he informed Scolex.

"God, you're irritating," Scolex answered, unconcerned. Gadget turned to RoboGadget. "And you're under arrest for impersonating a police officer."

"Get rid of him," Scolex told RoboGadget, who complied by punching Gadget out the back window. Gadget managed to grab the back bumper, and breathed a sigh of relief. Scolex thought for a moment, and then pushed a button. This released the bumper, sending Gadget tumbling end over end.

Gadget got up and watched as the limo rammed Gadgetmobile, shoving him into the bridge railing. Extending his legs to around fifteen feet, Gadget gave chase. Moments later he was literally on top of the limo. He leaned down and looked into the window, where Scolex and RoboGadget were whooping it up. RoboGadget pointed. Scolex turned and saw Gadget hanging upside down outside the window. He was shouting something at them that they couldn't hear. Then Gadget held his badge up to the window.

Scolex sighed and sent RoboGadget outside to finish off the inspector.

"You want him chopped or minced?" RoboGadget asked.

"Pureed," Scolex said with a sinister grin.

On top of the limo, RoboGadget grabbed Gadget's head and pushed it backward off his shoulders, just in time to see the traffic signal that knocked them both off the limo and onto the street. RoboGadget deployed his Gatling guns, firing at Inspector Gadget, who danced for his life.

When the limo skidded to a stop at the Scolex building, Sikes and Scolex climbed out of the car just in time to see Gadgetmobile bearing down on them.

"Nobody messes with the Gadgetmobile!" the car cried out, smashing into the limo. Brenda hopped out, and checked to make sure Gadgetmobile was all right.

"You!" she cursed at Scolex, marching toward him.

"Brenda, my love—" he started to say, as Brenda belted him with a right hook, sending him falling back into Sikes's arms. She pulled back for another, but Scolex caught her with his claw.

"Ow! Take that claw off me!" she demanded.

Still holding on to Brenda, Scolex turned to Sikes. "Get the foot," he ordered. "It's the only piece of evidence that links us to—" He suddenly remembered Brenda. "Brenda, Brenda, Brenda—I love it when you call me Claw," he said, dragging her into the building.

"So," he continued, trying to muster up some charm. "What's new?"

"Hello?" she wailed. "You killed my father!"

"Okay," he began, thoughtfully, "I realize we have some issues to work out, but Brenda, I love you."

Penny got off the bus in front of the Scolex building and ran up to Gadgetmobile.

"What happened to you?" she asked, noticing the damage.

"Nothing." The car shook off, all coolness. "What the heck are you doing here?"

"Evidence," she explained simply, and set off to find some.

Chapter

At the highest arch of the bridge tower, Gadget and RoboGadget prepared to square off. RoboGadget's hands turned into sickles as he advanced on Gadget, chopping mercilessly. Dodging this way and that, Gadget lost his balance, though he managed at the last second to grab something solid. It was a very long way down, Gadget thought, as he dangled off the bridge, swinging from RoboGadget's tie.

"Hey Gadget," RoboGadget said. "It's a clip-on." Gadget watched in horror as RoboGadget unclipped his tie.

"Aaaaaaaaa!" Gadget screamed, starting his free fall. But somehow he was able to find a piece of the bridge to grab on to, and when RoboGadget leaned over to see what had happened, Gadget yanked him forward. Now the two of them hung there, high above the traffic below, RoboGadget holding on to Gadget's pants for dear life.

* * *

Meanwhile Penny had found Sikes, who was in the process of trying to flush the foot down a toilet. Sikes was startled and pointed his gun at her.

Penny pretended not to be scared. "Why is your foot in the toilet?" she asked.

"Uh," Sikes replied, thinking as fast as he could, "I'm cleaning it."

"What's your name?" she asked.

"Sikes," he said. Penny studied him carefully.

"Well, Mr. Sikes," she summarized, "you don't look like the kind of a guy who should be blowing the head off a twelve-year-old girl. You look more like a guy who should be . . . helping someone pick out good weather stripping."

Sikes looked at her in amazement, then lowered his gun.

"My father has a hardware store," he said quietly, a single tear gliding down his cheek.

High above the city, a phone rang.

"Mine," Gadget informed his evil counterpart as they each checked their hand-phones. "Hello?"

"Is Penny there?" chimed two girlish voices in unison. Gadget recognized the voices as two of Penny's school chums.

"Nicole, Kim. Penny's not here. You can try her at home."

While Penny's uncle played answering machine,

RoboGadget acted. Opening his mouth wider than humanly possible (but easily possible for an evil android), he released the tarantula that had been built into his body. The deadly spider inched its way up Gadget's pant leg as he continued his phone call.

"Okay, I'll give her the message," he promised. "Rob and Skin are going to be at the mall. Got it. Bye." He hung up, puzzled by what he'd just heard.

"What do they mean they tried her at home and she's not there? And who the heck is Skin?" he demanded of no one in particular. And what was that crawling out of his sleeve? It looked like a big tarantul—

"Aaaaaaaahh!" Gadget yelled, losing his tenuous hold on the bridge as he tried to shake the spider off his hand. Gadget and RoboGadget plummeted toward the ground.

CRA-A-SH!! They landed in the back of a truck filled with shopping carts. The impact sent the carts flying in all directions, causing cars to skid and swerve to avoid them. Gadget and RoboGadget found themselves wedged into shopping carts which shot onto the highway. They continued fighting, extending their various limbs in an attempt to gain the upper hand while trying to free themselves from the shopping carts as they careened wildly through the oncoming traffic. *WHAM!* The cart slammed into a curb and tipped over, spilling Gadget and RoboGadget out on top of one another.

* * *

". . . And the next thing you know," Sikes confessed to Penny as they walked out of the secret lab, "you're a minion." Sikes was so relieved to finally have someone to talk to. Penny nodded sympathetically and gave his oversized hand an understanding pat.

Brain, meanwhile, had located Brenda on the roof of the Scolex Industries building and was attempting his own canine form of rescue—he was biting Scolex's leg! Scolex shook the little dog off violently, sending the brave beagle skidding back into a waiting elevator, the doors closing after him. With Sniffy in one hand and a claw-grip on Brenda, he headed across the roof to the helipad.

Gadget and RoboGadget untangled themselves and faced each other on the bridge.

"I've had it, pal," Gadget said angrily, removing his badge. "I'm not Inspector Gadget anymore, I'm just Gadget." He set his badge down and turned to face his opponent. "Get ready to RUMBL-L-L-LE!!"

Holding nothing back, Gadget charged full tilt straight at RoboGadget. Without breaking a sweat, *POW!* RoboGadget busted him in the face. Gadget shook off the blow and, showing no fear of his stronger and much meaner foe, immediately came at him again, extending his arm for a powerful jab. But before he could connect, RoboGadget grabbed his swinging arm and lifted Gadget over his head.

As Gadget struggled to break free, RoboGadget marched toward the side of the bridge, preparing to hurl Gadget to his doom. Gadget twisted his neck around looking around for some means of escape, something to latch on to, ANYTHING!

But there was nothing. Nothing but a ve-r-ry long drop and a little pin sticking out of the back of RoboGadget's neck. A pin? Gadget hadn't noticed that before. He looked closer. There was a small sign on the pin that read DO NOT PULL PIN. Gadget immediately pulled the pin.

SPROING!! RoboGadget's head ejected from his body, causing him to drop Gadget safely onto the bridge.

"Hey! What'd you do that for?" RoboGadget's head asked as it flew through the air. Gadget saw where it had landed and hurried over to see if it was dead.

"You killed me!" the head accused angrily.

"You should've quit while you were a head," Gadget quipped.

"Stuff it up your circuit breaker, Gadget!" the angry head retorted.

Gadget sighed.

"If there's one thing I can't stand," he declared, picking up the head and carrying it to the edge of the bridge, "it's an appliance with a dirty mouth." He tossed the head into the river, where it sank below the surface, never to cause evil again.

Gadget dusted off his hands and checked his

systems quickly. All in all, he was in pretty good shape after his battle with his evil twin. He turned and peered past the bridge to Scolex Industries, where Scolex was still at large.

"Go-Go-Gadget—Chopper!" he ordered. The Gadget Hat sprouted helicopter blades and lifted him into the air as the crowd on the bridge began to cheer.

Scolex assumed the controls of his helicopter in preparation for takeoff. Things weren't so bad, he thought. He had Sniffy, and he had Brenda, who was sure to love him when she had the opportunity to see his softer, tender side.

"I don't get it, Claw," she said, stalling for time as she tried to find a way to escape. "What's your plan now?"

"Since my dreams for a global robot empire hit the junk heap," he said, gazing at her recklessly, "I have only one obsession left."

"Lucky me."

"Sit back and relax, darling," Claw invited smoothly as he handcuffed her to the helicopter's control stick. "Soon we'll be sitting by the pool at my country estate in Uruguay."

"Two things, Scolex," Brenda said flatly. "One: You're insane. And Two: I liked you better *fat!*"

Scolex was initially stunned by her sudden outburst. Then it hit him. It hit him right in the pit of his slimmed-down stomach and he experienced a release unlike any he had ever experienced before.

"Bring on the brownies!" he cried out, joyous rapture on his face.

As long as he was distracted, Brenda yanked at her handcuffs, which jerked the controls hard left. The helicopter careened out of control, heading straight for the top of the building.

Scolex reacted just in time to avoid a collision as he swung the helicopter up and over the roof. He was just turning around to confront his misbehaving hostage when he was interrupted by an amplified voice.

"For the third time, Sanford Scolex," the voice boomed, "you are under arrest!"

Scolex couldn't believe what he was hearing. He looked up and was amazed to see Inspector Gadget and his Helicopter Hat hovering happily in front of him.

"This fellow will not give us a break!" Scolex growled, pushing a button on the control panel. A rocket shot out from the chopper and detonated in Gadget's hat, blowing its rotating blades to smithereens. Gadget fell to the roof below with a *THUD!*

Scolex quickly grabbed the control stick of the chopper and swooped in for the kill, but Gadget managed to roll aside and the chopper whooshed past him, missing by inches. Scolex circled around and came at him again. This time Gadget wasn't so lucky. As he tried to roll out of the way, his coat got caught on the helicopter's landing skids.

Gadget looked down as he hung suspended underneath the speeding chopper. They were headed for the city. Perhaps Scolex would drop him into a smokestack, or ram him into a building, or slice him into some high wires or—there seemed no end to the variety of ways Scolex could kill him.

He tried to calm himself. Then he remembered something he had learned not as Gadget, but as John Brown.

He reached into his coat pocket and calmly pulled out a ballpoint pen. Within seconds, he had field-stripped it, fashioning a crude firing mechanism from the spring assembly. He loaded the ink cartridge, aimed it at the chopper, and fired.

ZING! The cartridge sped through the air, right into the cockpit, where it ricocheted wildly before smashing into the "crush" button on Scolex's claw. *CRUNCH!* Before he knew what had happened, his claw had pulverized the helicopter's controls, allowing Brenda to slip her handcuffs off the stick. Scolex stared at his claw, stung by its betrayal.

POW! Brenda smacked Scolex square in the kisser, using the empty half of the handcuffs as a set of brass knuckles.

Two betrayals in as many seconds! This was not going well, Scolex thought, as the helicopter spun wildly out of control.

A slim chance of survival is better than none, thought Brenda, and she threw herself out of the chopper, landing right on Gadget's back. The impact tore his coat from the helicopter skid and sent them hurtling toward the ground.

"Go-Go-Gadget—Parachute!" John shouted. Nothing happened.

"Go-Go-Gadget—" His mind was racing. "Airbag!" he shouted hopefully. Nothing.

"I don't know what to Go-Go anymore," he admitted as they continued to fall. "Brenda," John said, looking into her eyes for what he was sure was the last time, "since we're most likely plummeting to our deaths, there's something I've been wanting to tell you for the longest time—"

"Okay," she agreed. "But first I have to put my hand in your shirt."

"I guess it can wait," he said.

She put her hand through the front of his shirt and reached around toward his spine, gently but quickly prodding it with her fingers.

"Ah!" she cried triumphantly as she found what she was looking for. She made a small adjustment to Gadget's back and a large umbrella deployed, immediately slowing their descent and causing them to start spinning slowly.

High above them, Scolex desperately attempted to bring his helicopter in for a safe landing, but it was no use. The smashed controls would not respond.

"Sniffy, jump!" he ordered. "Land on your feet! Save yourself!" Sniffy stared at him blankly.

"Good God, you're stupid," he observed. Then, acknowledging his own predicament, he added, "Aaaaaahhhhhhh!" as the helicopter continued to spin toward the ground.

Gadget and Brenda continued to descend slowly down toward the grounds of Scolex Industries. Gadget tried to maneuver them for a smooth landing, but bumped into the nose of a large statue of Scolex, which toppled to the ground with a loud *CRASH!* He also lost his grip on Brenda, and she landed with a *THUD* on the grass nearby. Gadget's landing was even less graceful—facedown. The impact deployed a colorful parachute, which billowed up and gently came to rest over the two of them.

Brenda knelt next to Gadget and turned him over to face her. His eyes were closed.

"Gadget, can you hear me?" she asked intently.

His eyes fluttered open and he saw her looking down at him.

"Hello, Brenda," he whispered, smiling woozily.

"Are you breathing?" she asked gently.

"I think so," he replied.

His hat had suddenly snapped to life, and the LED display was beginning to fizzle and crackle.

"How's your central vallecular equilibrator feel?" she asked tenderly.

"It feels okay," Gadget answered. But his hat displayed the message, YOU'RE BEAUTIFUL!

"And how's your auto-axle lubricator functioning?" Brenda continued, blushing slightly.

"It's fully functional," Gadget reported softly. But his hat displayed a series of hearts.

Now Brenda was positively beaming.

"Is your rotating auto-expanding hydro-pump fully charged?"

"It feels like it might just explode," he cautioned. But his hat said it all—I LOVE YOU.

"Oh, Gadget," she whispered, looking into his eyes.

"My Narvik 7 is beating so fast," he said, confused. "I don't remember reading anything in the manual about this."

"I guess we'll just have to write that chapter together." And with that, she touched her lips to his in a long, slow, wonderful kiss.

"Yaaaaaaaaaaaaahhhhhhhh!!!!," Scolex cried as he plummeted toward the earth, his pathetic excuse for a parachute barely slowing his descent.

On the ground below, Gadgetmobile had picked him up on his scope and was positioning himself to catch the hapless villain.

"Fly ball!" the car called, and a few seconds later Scolex landed in the backseat with a ground-shaking *THUMP!* He was followed by Sniffy, who landed with a lap-shaking *MEEEOWRR!* Happy to be alive, and instantly thirsting for revenge, the relentless robot-maker spoke his warning vow:

"This isn't adieu, Gadget!" he declared.

"I'd say it's bye-bye, baby," Gadgetmobile replied, as it converted the backseat into a neat little detention cage. Scolex scowled. Foiled by a fendered friend of his foe. He'd never live this down.

* * *

The police soon arrived. And the mayor. And the reporters. And the fire trucks. And the crowds. Penny arrived with Sikes and, with the foot as evidence, explained to Chief Quimby and anyone who would listen all about the evil RoboGadget and Scolex's failed master plan. Gadget was a hero once again, and the crowd cheered wildly for him. The next day Chief Quimby promoted him to inspector and promised to give him whatever cases his little Narvik 7 desired.

Scolex was found guilty at his trial and received multiple life sentences. Sikes, in light of his testimony and sincere remorse for his misguided ways, received probation on condition that he attend a twelve-step recovery program for former minions. Kramer spent many long weeks recuperating in a mental ward, but was finally released, with advice from his doctor that he take it easy and try to relax.

EPILOGUE

Penny watched Brain sleeping soundly nearby as she chatted with her friend Nicole on the new computer/phone/watch that Brenda had made for her. The household seemed calm compared to the excitement of the past few weeks, but she enjoyed the change.

Gadgetmobile sat in the driveway while Gadget and Brenda sat on the porch swing together, watching the stars.

Gadget kissed Brenda gently.

"Go-Go-Gadget," she whispered into his ear.

As he kissed her again, his toe rockets fired, lighting up the sky with a spectacular fireworks display.

"I'm on the case," he said.